STAR BABY

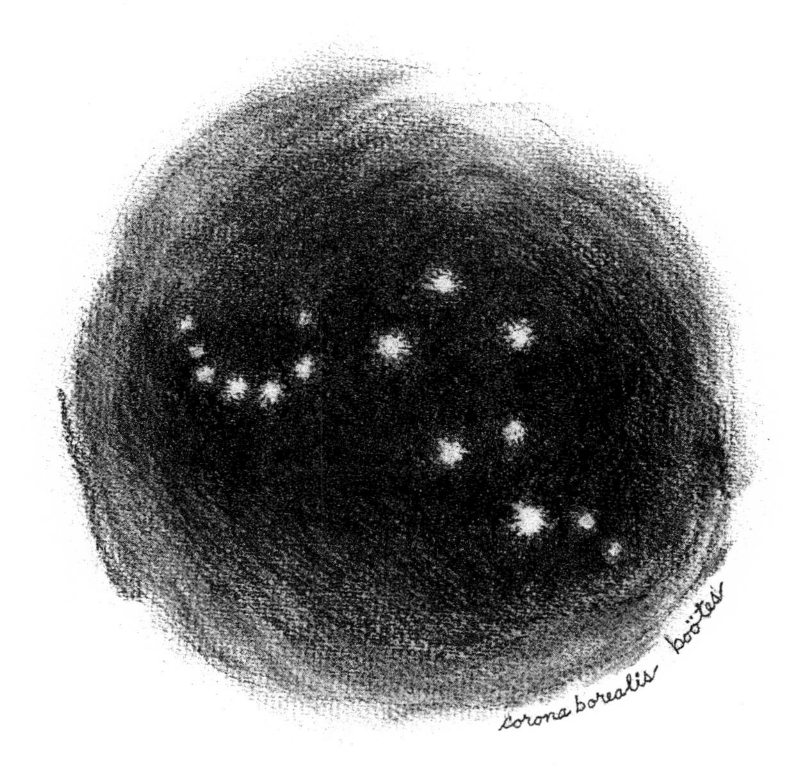

AMY LAWSON

pictures by
MARGOT APPLE

JANE YOLEN BOOKS
HARCOURT BRACE JOVANOVICH, PUBLISHERS
San Diego New York London

HBJ

Library of Congress Cataloging-in-Publication Data
Lawson, Amy.
Star baby/by Amy Lawson; pictures by Margot Apple. — 1st ed.
p. cm.
"Jane Yolen books."
Summary: Nine-year-old Allie, an only child, wishes on a falling star for a baby sister and receives a star baby instead.
ISBN 0-15-200905-1
[1. Extraterrestrial beings — Fiction. 2. Wishes — Fiction. 3. Brothers and sisters — Fiction.] I. Apple, Margot, ill. II. Title.
PZ7.L438228St 1992
[Fic] — dc20 90-36806

Designed by Lisa Peters
Printed in the United States of America
First edition A B C D E

for Mr. Kriebel,
who helped me photograph the moon
&
for my Star Babies,
Heidi, Nick, and Hugh

—A. L.

STAR BABY

Nine years old," said Poppa. "When you're nine years old, anything can happen."

My grandfather Poppa, Dad, and I were sitting at the table after supper waiting for Mom to bring in my birthday cake. Even though Poppa is blind, he seemed to be looking at me as he smiled.

"Nine is a magic number," he said. "When you're nine on the ninth day of the ninth month, all your birthday wishes come true."

"Honestly, Poppa," said Dad. "I wish you wouldn't talk like that in front of Allie. She'll start believing in all that stuff."

"I'm going to wish for a little sister," I said.

"Oh no," said Dad with a groan. "Not that old wish again."

"What did you expect? She's a Virgo, just like you," said Poppa as if that explained everything. Poppa knows a lot about astrology and he can tell all kinds of things about people because of it. "A little sister would be a fine thing for Allie, Henry," he added.

"I want a little sister so I won't be a Lonely Only," I said.

"A what?" asked Dad.

"A Lonely Only. Heather Vandergraf says Tommy Benson and I are Lonely Onlies because we don't have brothers and sisters. She says we're spoiled and can't roll with the punches."

"What punches?" asked Dad, looking worried.

"Heather has all these younger brothers and sisters, and she's always punching them," I said. "I guess that's what she means."

"You want a little sister so you can punch her?" Dad arranged the bread crumbs on his plate into a little circle. He likes things to be just so. Me too. Poppa says it's because we're Virgos and Virgos have to be neat.

"If I had a little sister, I wouldn't punch her." I stood up from the table so I could hang over Dad. "*Please,* Dad, won't you and Mom have another baby?"

Poppa sat, nodding his head and tapping his fingers on the table to a little tune he was humming. He always hums the same tune, an aria he calls it, a little song from an opera he likes.

Dad pushed his crumbs into a triangle. "You're so special, Allie. How could we possibly have another child as great as you?"

Mom poked her head in from the kitchen. There was a glop of frosting on her nose. Mom doesn't mind if things aren't just so. She's an Aries. Aries are free spirits, Poppa says.

"We can't have another baby because I'm too disorganized," Mom said. "It would be a disaster. Then you'd *never* have a birthday party."

I was going to have a real birthday party with all my friends, but, as usual, it would be a few days late. I didn't mind too much. It meant I always got two cakes.

"I can never even get the frosting to stick," said Mom, ducking back into the kitchen.

"Except to your nose," said Dad.

"Meteorite shower tonight," said Poppa in the middle of his hum. "Birthday present for you, Allie. All those falling stars for you to wish on."

"Now see, Allie," said Dad, turning his triangle into a square. "If we had a baby to take care of right now, we wouldn't be able to go out to see the stars with you tonight."

"You could take the baby. A baby would like all those stars," I started to say. Just at that moment, Mom came out and turned off the lights. As she held my cake, the burning candles danced in Poppa's glasses, which he wears even though he is blind.

"Happy birthday," Mom said.

Then Mom and Dad and Poppa sang. Even if I was a Lonely Only, right then I didn't mind. I loved how their voices mixed, and how Dad al-

ways looks embarrassed when he sings. There were nine candles and a big number nine right in the middle of the cake.

"Nine," Poppa whispered. His cheeks were apple-rosy above his red plaid shirt.

"Can you see the candles, Poppa?" I asked, because I know he can see a glow if the light is bright enough.

"No, but I can feel them," he said, putting his hand just above the flames. His fingers were like little animals, like moles sniffing the air and finding their way through the dark.

"Now make a wish, Allie," he said. "*Nueve, none, neuf, neun, nocto.* A magic spell to make your wish come true."

I made a wish inside myself and blew. As all nine candles flickered out, I thought that Poppa actually winked at me.

We went outside to watch the stars fall. Poppa sat on the blanket beside us. *Chirrup, chirrup,* the crickets were singing.

I shivered a little.

"It's too cold for September," Dad complained, putting on his old wool shirt.

There were so many stars I had to stretch my eyes to see them all. If I stared hard, the stars blurred together to make one big star. Then *streak!* Quick! I saw one fall, a bright little lizard in the black sky.

"There! And there! And there's another one!" I shouted. "Oh, Poppa, I wish you could see."

"I hear the crickets, Allie," he said, taking my hand. His moley fingers felt warm and dry. "And the air smells of clover and chives."

"There's the Big Dipper," said Dad, lying on his back. "And the North Star, and Cassiopeia in her chair."

"I can never figure out the constellations," Mom complained. "It's all just a mess of stars to me."

"See, up *there,* Rachel," said Dad, impatient. "Start with the North Star."

"And you always *point,* as if I could tell what you're pointing to," Mom grumbled.

"Well, then, look at the Milky Way," said Dad. "All those billions and billions of stars — those you can see."

"Like a blanket of stars," said Mom.

"Like a ribbon," I put in.

"Those are babies," said Poppa.

Dad sat up with a grunt. "*Now* what kind of story is he going to tell us?"

"It's called the Milky Way because the babies up there are drinking milk."

I giggled and squeezed Poppa's arm. It was fun to look up and think that all those stars were babies.

"Go on, Poppa, what else about the babies?"

"Do you know what constellations are, Allie? They're heroes, like Orion and Samson and Hercules, or princesses and queens like Andromeda and Cassiopeia." Poppa's voice doesn't sound as old as the rest of him, especially when he is telling a story. "Well, of course those heroes and princesses and queens have babies, and they're growing up there in the sky."

"The trouble is, he believes all this stuff," said Dad.

"Do you, Poppa?" Before he went blind, sometimes he'd get a smile in his eyes. Now it was hard to tell what he did believe. "Look at that!" I shouted suddenly. "A star is falling, Poppa, but slowly, slowly, leaving a long white tail."

"Then it's a wishing star," said Poppa. "When a star falls slowly, you make a wish."

I wish, I said inside myself. *I wish . . .*

The star was still falling, and it fell, and it fell — oh, it was so bright, and it was coming right toward us. Do you think we could move? We sat on the blanket, frozen, with our mouths hanging open — until — *it was right over our heads!* It spun in the air, a white light spitting sparks of red and blue and yellow.

Poppa half stood with his arms outstretched. "What is it?" he cried. "I see a light. What is it?"

Then everything went spooky black. Even the crickets were quiet. It was so quiet I think for a moment the earth stopped spinning.

Something dropped into Dad's arms.

Something cried, "*Wah! Wah! Wah!*"

"Oh my," Dad croaked. "It's raining babies."

Mom whispered, "A baby!"

Poppa shouted with joy and leapt into the air. "I knew it, I knew it, I knew it," he cried, his voice going on in the dark like some kind of night bird.

In the dim light I could see a lump wriggling in Dad's arms. It *was* a baby. I felt awfully creepy, bumps on my arms, pricks on my neck, tears in my eyes. After all, I had made the same wish two times tonight, and here . . .

"Wah! Wah! Wah!" cried the baby.

"I think it's hungry," said Mom.

"Of course," said Poppa. "It misses its milk. And probably it's scared, too. Wouldn't you be if you had just fallen from the Milky Way? Take it into the house, Henry."

"You take it, Rachel," said Dad. Poor Dad. He was shaking all over.

Mom stood, picked up the blanket, and wrapped it around the baby. We walked into the house. Dad grabbed Poppa and held on to him as if *he* were the one who needed to be helped.

"Warm up some milk, Henry," said Mom as she pushed open the kitchen door. She sat in the rocker, cradling the baby in her arms. "Allie, look in the closet and see if you can find an old bottle and some diapers."

I looked in the closet, through one hundred pairs of mittens and a thousand years' worth of Christmas wrapping paper. Mom never throws anything away.

"Wah! Wah! Wah!" cried the baby.

"Oh dear," said Mom, rocking and rocking, "I thought we were all finished with this."

"We are," said Dad, pacing around the kitchen. "We are not keeping this — this — little chunk of matter that fell through the earth's atmosphere."

"Here's a bottle, Dad," I said, pulling one out from one of my old boots.

"There you go, Star Baby," said Mom when the bottle was washed and the milk was warmed. "Everything's going to be all right now." She spoke in a whispery singsong.

I stood in a corner all alone. I felt like more of a Lonely Only than I'd ever felt before.

"Henry, it's so *cute,*" said Mom. She was staring into the baby's face. "Poppa, I wish you could see — it is *so* cute."

Dad and Poppa stood behind Mom. Poppa put out a hand above the baby's face, just as he had with the candles.

"Ah," Poppa sighed. "Light."

I crept closer. The baby did seem to glow.

"Oh, Allie, the Star Baby's a boy," said Mom suddenly. "He could be a little brother for you."

Then I was dizzy. Everything seemed to turn sideways. I sat down on the floor with a thud.

A little brother? That was not what I asked for.

"Yuck!" I was beginning to cry. "I don't want a dumb baby that fell from the sky."

Dad sat on the floor next to me and put his arm around me. "Neither do I," he said.

"Gurgle gurgle coo," said the baby, smiling at Mom.

"But where will he go if we don't keep him?" asked Mom.

"Go?" asked Poppa. "He just *got* here—and we haven't even said hello."

He found one of the baby's fingers. "How do you do, Star Baby? Welcome to Earth."

When I woke up the next morning, I went into Mom and Dad's room. They were still sleeping. Next to their bed was a small basket, the one I had slept in when I was a baby.

I looked in it. The basket was empty. Where was the baby? Could he have gone back up to the sky? Then I heard him.

"Gurgle gurgle coo."

I looked up. There was the baby, bobbing on the

ceiling like a balloon. He was laughing and batting the air with his fists.

I jumped up onto the bed. "Mom, Dad, look at the baby."

"Ooooooh, the baby," said Mom, groaning. "Now I remember why I didn't want to do this all over again." She rolled over and looked in the basket. "Allie, what have you done with the baby?" She sat up frowning, her hair flying in fifty directions.

"Mom, look up." I pointed to the ceiling.

Mom looked up. Her mouth dropped open.

"Henry, wake up." Mom shook Dad's shoulder. Dad grunted. He was lying on his back.

"Good grief," he said as he opened his eyes. "Please make it go away." He pulled the covers over his head.

"But, Henry," said Mom, "he's so adorable. Look, even Allie likes him now."

The Star Baby was making me laugh so hard I nearly fell off the bed.

Dad's nose poked out from under the covers. "Has it gone yet?" he asked.

"I'm getting Poppa," I yelled.

I ran into Poppa's room and gently shook his arm.

"Poppa, Poppa, it's me, Allie. The Star Baby's on the ceiling. I wish you could see."

After Poppa put in his teeth, I dragged him into Mom and Dad's room. Dad was standing on the bed peering up at the Star Baby. He had the scientific look on his face he gets when something is really interesting to him. Mom was lying on her back staring up with a huge smile.

"Good morning, Star Baby," said Poppa, turning his face to the ceiling. He seemed to know just where to look.

"Gurgle gurgle coo," said the Star Baby.

Dad reached up gently and pulled the Star Baby down.

"Henry, why do you suppose he floats like that?" asked Mom.

"Stars are made of helium and hydrogen, gases that are lighter than air," said Dad, frowning as he tried to think. "Maybe he's full of helium and hydrogen."

"Maybe he's full of milkonium," said Poppa with a smile.

"Milkonium?" said Dad suspiciously. "You're just making that up." He let go of the Star Baby. Up the baby popped, right back to the ceiling. Dad sat down on the bed, shaking his head.

"I want to do that. I want to play with the Star Baby," I shouted, jumping onto the bed. I stood between Dad and Mom and tried to grab the baby's leg.

"Oh, Allie, he'll be so much fun for you," said Mom.

"Rachel," said Dad, looking at Mom and turning quite pale.

"Henry," said Mom, setting her lips. She stood so she could pull the Star Baby down and hold him in her arms.

"Look," said Dad. "How do you know he even wants to be here? Maybe he misses all the other Star Babies up there. Oh help," he said, clutching his hair. "How can I be talking like this?"

Mom sat down with the Star Baby. As I snuggled next to her, I stared at the Star Baby's fingers. They were so pink and new, like baby mice.

"Don't you think he's cute, even if he is a boy?" asked Mom.

"Well," I said. "Maybe we could just try him out for a while, and if we don't like him, we can send him back."

"Allie," said Mom. "You don't do that with babies."

"But maybe," said Poppa, "maybe with Star Babies, that *is* what you do."

"Whether we keep him or not, he's with us for right now," said Mom. "So we need to give him a name."

"How about Total Disaster," said Dad. "Or Metie, short for Meteorite."

"He's not a Meteorite," said Poppa thoughtfully rubbing his face. "He's a Star Baby, the son of a hero like Samson or Jason or Hercules."

"Jason and Samson aren't constellations, Poppa," Dad said.

"Of course they are," said Poppa.

"Samson, Jr.," Mom suggested.

"No way," I said, thinking of Heather Vandergraf and Tommy Benson. "If he has a dumb name he'll get picked on."

"How about Sammy?" asked Poppa, reaching for the Star Baby's hand. "Hey, Sammy, how do you like that for a name?"

"Gurgle gurgle coo," said Sammy with a smile.

"Good," said Poppa. "Then Sammy it is."

"Let's take Sammy for a walk," said Mom. "Where do you suppose I put all your old clothes, Allie? And where's the stroller? Oh dear, I *knew* I was too disorganized to have another baby."

"I'm going to work," said Dad. "Maybe when I get home, none of this will have happened."

An hour later, Sammy was ready for a walk. Mom let me push the stroller, while she and Poppa walked beside us, arm in arm.

"Mom, don't you think Sammy's grown a lot since last night?" I asked.

"He does seem bigger," said Mom thoughtfully. "Maybe it's just seeing him by the light of day."

"Goo," said Sammy, laughing and waving his arms. He seemed to be having a good time.

"Uh-oh, here comes Tommy Benson," I said, looking down the road.

"Uh-oh, here comes Tommy Benson's *mother,*" said Mom. "For right now, let's pretend Sammy is not a star."

"Why, hello Rachel, hello Poppa, hello Allie," said Mrs. Benson. "And whom do we have here?" she asked, bending down to look at Sammy.

"This is Sammy," said Poppa proudly. "Our Star Baby."

"Your Star Baby?" asked Mrs. Benson, looking confused. "Why, Rachel, I didn't even know you were expecting."

"She wasn't expecting," said Poppa. "She was surprised." He chuckled. "We all were."

"He's sort of adopted," said Mom.

"He dropped from the sky," said Poppa.

"You know what he means," said Mom, nervously trying to push by Mrs. Benson. "It all happened so suddenly."

"I just adore babies," said Mrs. Benson, bending close to Sammy again.

"Gah," said Sammy, his face puckering as if he might cry.

"Tommy, come look," said Mrs. Benson. "Don't you think this is just the cutest baby?"

Tommy folded his eyelids up so the pink underneath showed, making him look as if he had pink eyes.

"This baby is so sweet, I'm going to have to pick him up," said Mrs. Benson. With a flick of her wrists, she began to undo the straps of the stroller.

"Oh no!" Mom cried.

"Now, don't you worry," said Mrs. Benson, turning to Mom. "I just — "

Sammy floated right up into the top branches of an oak tree. It was the tallest tree for miles around.

"Did she?" asked Poppa.

"She did," Mom wailed.

"Cool," Tommy whispered. His eyelids flipped back down. "That baby just flew away."

Mrs. Benson clutched Mom's arm. "What kind of baby *is* that?"

"A Star Baby," said Mom. She had tears in her eyes. "And we might not ever see him again."

We heard a giggling from the top of the tree. I caught a glimpse of Sammy.

"He's okay, Mom," I said. "He's just tangled in the branches. I'll climb up and get him."

"I'll climb," said Tommy.

Tommy and I both clawed at the bottom of the tree. We couldn't even reach the lowest branches.

"A cat couldn't climb up there," Tommy grumbled, kicking the tree.

"Call the fire department," Poppa suggested. "They're always rescuing things from trees."

"But *babies?"* said Mom.

"Come on, dear, *I'll* call the fire department," said Mrs. Benson, taking Mom by the arm. She seemed over the shock. "Mr. Benson is a volunteer firefighter and he'll know what to do. Come on, dear, you must be brave."

"Allie, you stay here and keep an eye on Sammy," Mom called as Mrs. Benson hurried her away.

"I'll stay, too," said Tommy. "That's a cool baby. Where'd you get him?"

Poppa sat down with his back against the tree as I thought about whether or not I would tell Tommy about the falling star and how I'd made a wish that had mostly come true.

"I'm going to get a Star Baby, too," said Tommy. "Only mine will be better."

Poppa was humming his aria and Sammy was shouting baby laughs from the top of the tree. I decided to keep my mouth shut. I wasn't going to tell Tommy Benson anything.

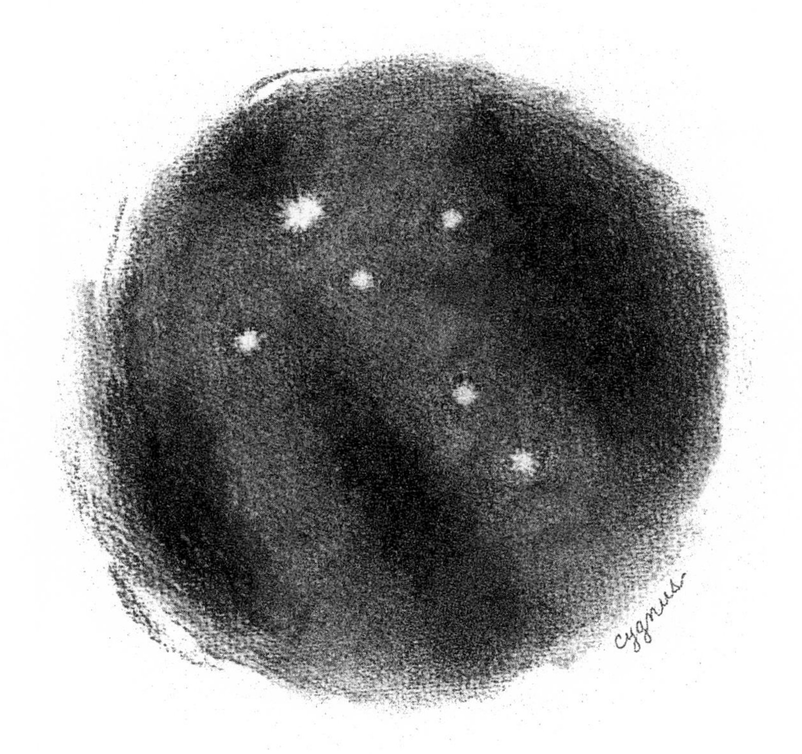

Mom and Mrs. Benson finally came back.

"Lemonade and cookies," said Mrs. Benson brightly, opening the basket she was carrying. She set down the basket and poured a drink for Poppa.

"A cool head in a crisis. You must be a Pisces," said Poppa.

Before Mrs. Benson could answer, we heard the fire trucks.

"I told them it was a three-alarm fire," said Mrs. Benson.

"Wait until they find out it's a three-alarm *baby,*" said Mom, pacing nervously in front of the tree.

The fire trucks roared up the road. All the fire trucks in our town came and all the firefighters, plus a couple from the neighboring town. All the police cars came, and all the neighbors. Mr. Benson, Tommy's father, was standing on the back of a truck clanging a bell.

"Wah! Wah! Wah!" cried Sammy up in the tree.

"I think you're scaring the baby," said Mom, pointing up to the leaves.

"The WHAT?" said all the firefighters at once, and all the police, *and* all the neighbors. Poppa just sat at the bottom of the tree with a smile on his face, humming his little tune.

"Can you please get my baby down?" asked Mom. She looked as though she might cry. She pointed to the top of the tree again. "Please hurry. I'm so afraid he might float away."

Everyone stared at Mom. No one said a word.

"Gurgle gurgle coo." Sammy's little voice drifted down through the leaves.

Everyone jumped, pointing and waving. "A

BABY!" they all yelled at once in different sorts of voices.

"Isn't it *wonderful?*" Mrs. Benson gushed, as if Sammy were *her* baby.

Mr. Benson jumped off the truck and walked up to Mom. He stood at attention in front of her as if he were a soldier. "Leave it to me, Rachel. You'll have your baby. A fireman never shirks his duty, no matter how weird." He saluted Mom and then patted her on the shoulder. "Excuse me, sir," he yelled over to Poppa. "You're going to have to move. Come on, men, bring the ladder over here."

Mr. Benson leaned the ladder against the tree, and then he climbed and climbed until all we could see of him were the bottoms of his boots.

"It's okay, baby," we heard him say. "Don't be scared, little baby, everything's going to be fine."

"Isn't he *brave?*" Mrs. Benson gushed.

"Coming down," Mr. Benson shouted. First his boots and his pants appeared, and then Sammy, held tightly against his chest.

"Goo goo gurgle gurgle goo," Sammy chortled.

Everyone gasped and then cheered.

3

"I want one," Tommy began to whine. "I want a Star Baby right now."

"That's enough, Tommy," said Mr. Benson, handing Sammy to Mom. "And here's your baby, Rachel, safe and sound."

What about my birthday party? It's tomorrow and we haven't done anything for it yet," I said to Mom that night as she was getting Sammy ready for a bath. She was going to put him in the kitchen sink, just the way she used to give me a bath.

"Do you really want a birthday party?" she asked, unbuttoning Sammy's overalls. "Don't you think we've had enough excitement for a while?"

"Yes, I do want a party and I can't tell my friends

not to come. Anyhow, I'm sure they've all bought me presents already."

"Maybe they could just drop by one at a time," said Mom vaguely. "Just think, Sammy, we almost lost you today." She peeled off his diaper.

"*Mom,* you're changing the subject." I was beginning to get mad.

"Come read the day's horoscopes to me, Allie," said Poppa in a calm voice from the kitchen table. "What does mine say?"

I sat down next to Poppa with a sigh and picked up the newspaper.

"Pay close attention to family matters," I read. "Those around you need you more than ever."

"That's for sure," Poppa exclaimed. He chuckled. "It's amazing how these horoscopes are always right."

"Huh—that nonsense!" said Dad with a grunt, as he came into the kitchen. "How can you believe that stuff?"

"Just think, Henry, we almost lost Sammy today," said Mom again.

"Maybe we should have," Dad grumbled. He sat

down at the table and spread the rest of the paper before him.

"Don't be so mean, Henry," said Mom. "I'm just getting used to having a baby again."

"I'm not being mean," said Dad. "I've been thinking about things, that's all. I'm not convinced this baby is ours to keep. What happens when his parents realize he's gone? Next thing you know, we'll have a bunch of constellations down here looking for him." Dad shuddered and shook the newspaper. "And then I'll *really* lose my mind."

"I suppose you're right," said Mom sadly. She tucked Sammy under an arm as she turned on the water. "Maybe we should bundle him up right now and let him float home. What do you think, Poppa?"

"Give him a bath and then decide," said Poppa. "Can't send the baby home dirty."

"That's true," said Mom, looking relieved. "In you go, Sammy. We've got you for a little longer." She turned off the water and lifted him into the sink. "Oof! I swear he has gained ten pounds since he's been here. Look how much bigger he is."

"Goo," said Sammy with a smile. He slapped the water so it splashed into Mom's face.

"No, no, Sammy," said Mom. "No splashing, and you stay put," she added, putting a hand on Sammy's shoulder as he began to float up.

"Gurgle gurgle coo," cried Sammy, kicking his feet.

"Sammy, you're getting me soaking wet!" Mom shouted. As she reached for a towel, she let go of him. There was a noise, like a rushing of air. Then Sammy was in the air, his arms, legs, chest, and tummy blowing up as if he were a fancy balloon.

Dad almost fell out of his chair. Mom froze where she was standing, towel in the air.

"He's a blimp," Mom croaked as Sammy rose higher and higher.

"He's a whale," whispered Dad.

"What's going on?" asked Poppa. He rubbed a hand through his hair. "Why is it raining in here?" Sammy was floating above him, dripping water all over the kitchen.

"Sammy's in the air and he's growing," I shouted. I leapt around beneath him, trying to grab him. His

hands were as big as baseball mitts. He was laughing and clapping them together.

"Helium doesn't expand in heat," said Dad, looking puzzled.

"Milkonium does," said Poppa.

"Oh, do you really think so?" asked Dad. His face had its serious, scientific expression.

Sammy was getting bigger and bigger. I was suddenly scared he would explode. I ducked under the kitchen table. "I don't want Sammy to pop," I wailed.

"It's okay, Allie," said Mom. "He's beginning to shrink now. He's cooling off."

I crawled out from under the table. Mom was right. Sammy was looking more like a baby again and floating back down. He landed right in Dad's arms.

"You're just full of tricks, aren't you, Star Baby?" said Dad, smiling into Sammy's face. "What would happen to you if we put you into the freezer?"

"Henry!" exclaimed Mom in a shocked voice.

"Coo!" said Sammy with a giggle. He wriggled out of Dad's arms and jumped to the floor. He spread out his arms, pitched forward on his toes, and toddled straight towards Mom. *"Sczoom!"* he yelled. He butted his head right into her knees.

"He didn't float," whispered Mom.

"He *walked,*" croaked Dad.

"How come?" I asked.

"He's a hero's son, that's all," said Poppa calmly. "I suppose pretty soon he'll be able to do anything he wants."

"Come to Daddy, Sammy." Dad knelt on the floor and opened his arms. Sammy turned and hurled himself at him. Back and forth, back and forth, Sammy ran between Dad and Mom.

"Hey," I said, suddenly sick of Sammy. "Doesn't anyone care I'm supposed to have a birthday party tomorrow and we haven't done anything about it?"

Mom brushed the hair out of her eyes. She was a mess. Her sweater was soaking wet and her blouse was untucked.

"I'm sorry, Allie," she said. "It's just that with Sammy, I haven't had time to think about it."

"Mom, you *are* too disorganized to have another baby."

"Allie," said Dad, frowning at me.

"We're sending Sammy back home now, aren't we?" I asked.

Mom sighed. "I guess we should get him ready to go."

Dad sighed, too. He picked up Sammy and wrapped a towel around him. "Somebody up there must be missing him a lot. He sure is a dandy baby."

"I just remembered the weather report," said Poppa. "It's supposed to rain tonight. Outside, I mean," he added, feeling his wet hair with his fingers. "I don't think you should send him up just yet. It might be an uncomfortable trip in the rain. Not something I'd like to do."

"No," said Dad thoughtfully. He seemed to be holding Sammy awfully tight.

"No," agreed Mom. "If he caught a cold, what would they say up there about us down here?"

"What's wrong with a little rain?" I grumbled. "He can wear my rain hat. He can take my umbrella."

"Hush, Allie," said Mom, taking Sammy from Dad. "Sammy's falling asleep. He's had an exciting day. Let's find some pajamas and put him to bed."

"Come on, Allie," said Poppa, as Mom and Dad went upstairs with Sammy. "Let's read your horoscope."

The newspaper was wet from Sammy dripping on it, but I could still read it.

"You're not going to believe this one, Poppa," I said.

"Sure I will. I'll believe anything," said Poppa. "Go ahead, what does it say?"

"An unexpected visitor will change your life," I read.

"Ha!" Poppa exclaimed. "I told you horoscopes are always right."

The next afternoon the doorbell rang.

"Uh-oh," said Mom, looking panicky. "Your party's beginning and I haven't even finished the cake."

Tommy Benson was at the door. "Where's the Star Baby?" he asked right off. He didn't say happy birthday, and he didn't hand me a present.

"He's in the kitchen," I said. Mom and Dad still hadn't sent Sammy home. They said it was too windy. I pretended to yawn. "Sammy is pretty boring, actually."

"I think he's cool," said Tommy. He pushed past me to run into the kitchen.

Heather Vandergraf arrived. I thought we should stay in the living room and have the party in there and not even have to see Sammy at all, but Heather said, "Where's the Star Baby?" She didn't say happy birthday, and she dropped my present on the floor. She shouldered her way into the hall.

"In there," I said, pointing to the kitchen. "But it'll cost you a dollar." She didn't even hear me, or if she did, she didn't get the joke.

Ben, Jane, Hilary, and Matthew arrived.

Ben didn't have his present with him. He must have been in such a hurry to see Sammy, he forgot it at home.

Jane was wearing an old shirt, jeans, and dirty sneakers. Usually she wore frilly dresses, white socks, and shiny black shoes to birthday parties. "So, where's that baby?" she asked.

Hilary ran into the house screaming, "Where is

he?" at the top of her lungs. Hilary never screamed or shouted. She was quiet and shy. We always made her play the dead person when we put on plays.

Matthew, who was standing behind Hilary when she came in, ducked around to the back door. He must have figured he could get to Sammy faster if he didn't have to get by me first.

Not one person wished me a happy birthday. Only Heather brought me a present, and she didn't even hand it to me.

I went into the kitchen. Mom and Dad and Poppa and all the kids were in there. Sammy was on the ceiling. Sammy's eyes were bright. He was clapping his hands, saying something that sounded like "Yaaaay!"

"I should have brought my butterfly net," said Tommy excitedly. "How do you get him down?"

"He's not a butterfly," said Poppa gently. "He's a Star Baby. Let him be."

"Look!" Heather screamed. "He's coming down all by himself."

"How does he do that?" Dad wondered. "He's like a hot air balloon."

"*Like* a balloon," Poppa said, "but not a balloon. He's a Star Baby."

"Look," said Ben, jumping up and down. "He's playing Loop-the-loop."

Sammy floated up and then turned a somersault in the air.

"HOLY COW!" Hilary screamed.

"Not a cow," said Poppa, but I was the only one who heard him.

Sammy flipped one more time and when everyone clapped, he clapped too and giggled and said, "YAAAAAY!" Then he floated down.

When he landed, he ran as hard as he could straight toward us. At the last minute he seemed to hold his breath. Up he floated, instead of crashing.

"YAAAAAAY!" he squealed while everyone laughed and clapped.

There was no question about it: Sammy was showing off, and Sammy was ruining my birthday party!

"I want everyone to go home now," I yelled. I ran out of the kitchen, slammed the door, and ran up to my bedroom, shouting: "THE LAST THING IN

THE WORLD I EVER WANTED WAS A STUPID LITTLE STAR BABY BROTHER."

Mom came up to talk to me. She tried to joke. "At least we had some entertainment," she said. "I didn't have to hire a clown. And no one cared that we didn't have any balloons."

"*Sammy* was the balloon," I wailed. I buried my head into the pillow.

Dad came up to talk to me. He tried to be serious. "You weren't very nice to your friends," he said.

"I don't care," I said from under the pillow. "I don't have any friends. No one brought me a present except for Heather and she dropped it on the floor. They all came to see Sammy — not me."

Next I heard Poppa's shoes scuffing along the hallway. He stuck his head into my room. "Tough having a little brother, isn't it?" he said.

I came out from under the pillow. Poppa stood there looking thoughtful as he rubbed a hand across his face.

"It's terrible, Poppa," I said.

"But I thought that's what you wanted."

"I wanted a *sister*."

"Brother, sister, you think it makes such a big difference?"

I sat up. "No, I guess not," I said. I wanted Poppa to come in and sit down on my bed and hold my hand in his big moley fingers and tell me it was time for Sammy to go home, but Poppa stayed just outside my door.

"Mom loves having a baby again, and Dad, who *said* he didn't want another baby, is so proud of Sammy, of every new thing he does. They'll never want him to go home," I said, beginning to sniff.

"How about an Earth Baby?" asked Poppa. "Would an Earth Baby be better than a Star Baby?"

I sat and thought. I didn't know for sure, but I thought it might be best just to be a Lonely Only.

"Well, you think about that one," said Poppa. He shut my door and shuffled away. I could hear him humming his little tune.

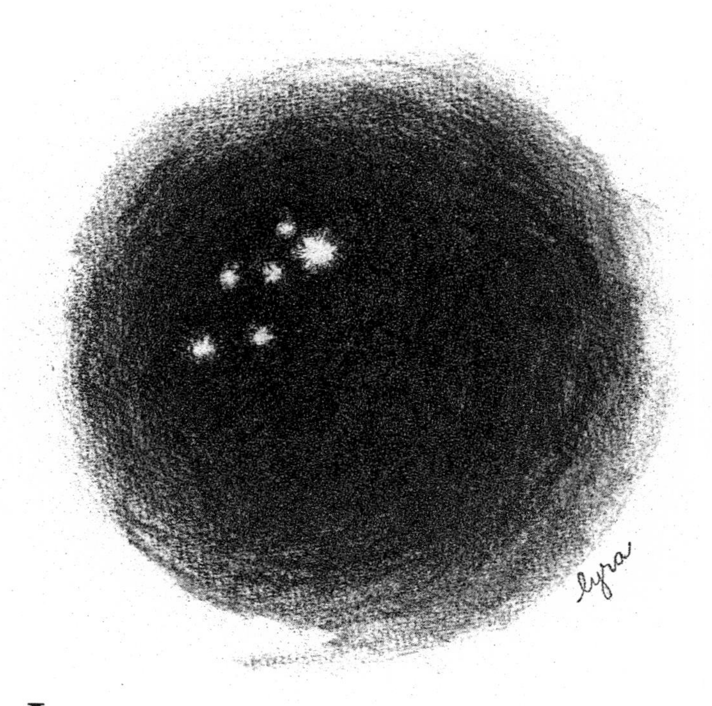

I fell asleep. When I woke up, Sammy was sitting on my bed.

"Allie, are you asleep?" he asked.

I blinked my eyes. I couldn't believe my ears. Sammy still looked like a baby, but he was talking like a kid.

"I want to go outside and go floating with you." He spoke in a gruff little voice.

"What?" I said, sitting up in bed. "How?"

"Come on," said Sammy. He held my hand as we

went outside. I had never held his hand before. His little mice fingers were warm and soft. He started to run.

"Hold on, Allie," he cried.

I held on. Up, up, up we went above the bushes, above the trees. Thump, thump, thump, my heart beat fast. I was an owl swooping beneath the moon. The meadows looked just like the quilt on my bed except there were cows sleeping in the patches.

"This is fun, Allie," said Sammy, turning his head to look at me. "I like floating with you. And I'm sorry if I wrecked your birthday party," he added in his gruff voice.

"I like floating with you, too, Sammy," I said. I cleared my throat and squeezed his hand. "And I guess I'm not mad at you anymore." How could I be mad at a talking baby who took me floating above the fields? I started to giggle, and then we both laughed really hard.

We floated through a warm patch, and then a cool one. It was just like swimming except I didn't have to move my arms and legs.

"Let's go wake up Tommy Benson," I said. I

started to giggle again. "Won't he be mad if I can float and he can't?"

We drifted toward Tommy Benson's house and then hung in the air outside his bedroom window.

"He looks better with his eyes shut," I said, looking in. "He even has a teddy bear tucked in with him. Yoo-hoo, Tommy!" I tapped on his window.

Tommy shot out of bed. He blinked, rubbing his eyes. When he saw us, he began to howl, "Mommy! Daddy! There's a two-headed monster trying to get in my window."

"Tommy," I half whispered, half shouted. "It's us, Sammy and Allie."

Tommy padded toward us slowly, clutching his teddy bear. Then he opened the window.

"Look, Tommy, Sammy took me floating," I said.

"Cool," said Tommy, completely awake now. He stuck a hand out the window and grabbed one of Sammy's arms. "How'd you do that? I wanna do that."

The next thing I knew, Sammy, Tommy, Tommy's teddy bear, and I were floating. This was *not* what I had meant to have happen.

"This is *soooooooo* cool," said Tommy. His eyes were gleaming in the moonlight.

"I want to go up," said Sammy suddenly in his gruff little voice.

"He's talking, too," said Tommy. "What a baby!"

"How up?" I asked. I couldn't help yawning and I wasn't sure how much longer I could hold on.

"To the stars up," said Sammy.

"The stars are a long, long way, Sammy," I explained. "It would take us a long time to get there."

I felt pricks of panic on the back of my neck as we began to rise. Did Sammy think he could take us all the way to the Milky Way? Down below, the houses were getting smaller and smaller.

"I want to play with my brothers and sisters," said Sammy. "I miss them." The stars above seemed to be growing larger.

"You can play with me," I said. "You just said you liked floating with me."

"I like you a lot," said Sammy. He sighed, and his face looked sad in the moonlight. "But up there, all of us are together. We play games and sing. Come on, I can show you."

"Yeah, come on," said Tommy. "Then I can get a Star Baby of my own."

"Tommy!" I yelled. I was so scared I almost let go of Sammy. "We can't go to the Milky Way. It's too far."

"If he could come down here, we can go up there," said Tommy.

"That's different," I started to say. "*He's* different."

Sammy was kicking his legs, and we shot up, faster and faster.

When you're in a stink, think. That's what Poppa always says. I shut my eyes and tried to think, and I thought of three things.

One was: What if we *could* go up — Sammy, Tommy, and I — all the way to the Milky Way? Once we were up there, could we get back down? I sure didn't want to be stuck up there forever.

The second thing was: What if we went back down and let Sammy go home by himself? The trouble was that now I really didn't want him to go — even if he was a boy, even if I had to share him with Mom and Dad, even if he had wrecked my birthday party. Every day was exciting with him. Floating was fun. And I liked the way his little mice fingers curled inside my hand.

All that was left was the third thing.

"Sammy," I said as the lights below grew into faint little stars on land, "if we could get another Star Baby to come down and play with you, would you like to stay here on Earth?"

Sammy wriggled in the air. He frowned for a moment and then his eyes shone — twinkled — like stars. "Oh yes!" he cried. "That would be fun."

"Cool," said Tommy. "That's a much better idea. And it's my turn to get a Star Baby."

"Go down now," I ordered Sammy. I was dizzy and finding it hard to breathe. I had once learned that the higher you are, the less air there is, and now I knew it was true. And it was cold.

Sammy pulled up his knees just as if he were slamming on the brakes. We drifted for a moment and then he began to pull us down.

"Not too fast, Sammy," I said. "My ears are popping." Besides, I needed time to think because I was still in a stink. And what I was thinking was that I did not want Tommy Benson to have a Star Baby.

What would happen if I wished for another Star Baby? I shook my head as we began to be able to see meadows again. Another Star Baby would be a Total Disaster for Mom. As for Dad, he would never have *any* time for me anymore. He'd always be with the Star Babies.

And Poppa would say, "What? You asked for *another* Star Baby? Isn't one enough?" He'd think I was being greedy.

We hit the ground with a thud. When I tried to walk, my legs were shaky and my fingers felt as though they wanted to stay curled around Sammy's hand forever.

"Okay, Allie, tell me how to get one." Tommy was hanging over me like a vulture.

"All right," I said slowly. I didn't know what else to do. "But if I tell you how to get a Star Baby, you have to promise not to be mean to it."

"I won't be mean," said Tommy. "He'll be my best friend."

"He? How do you know it'll be a *he?* You might get a girl."

"Yeah," said Sammy excitedly. "I hope we get one of the girls."

Tommy was still for a moment. "Then *she'll* be my best friend." He grinned and looked so happy even the freckles on his nose seemed to bounce.

"Okay then," I said. "Look for a falling star, and when you see one, wish for a baby. Only don't say your wish out loud."

Tommy, Sammy, and I sat on the grass looking up at the stars. It made me think of how — just a short time ago — Mom and Dad and Poppa and I sat outside, the night that Sammy fell.

"You know what?" said Tommy, suddenly sitting up very straight. "Every time a star falls, I can wish for *another* Star Baby."

"Oh no," I groaned. "You can't do that."

"Why not?" he asked. He jumped up, waving his arms excitedly. "Boy! Wouldn't that be fun! Can you picture the look on Mom's face?"

"I wonder how *my* mom is," said Sammy suddenly scrambling to his feet. "And my dad. I wonder

if they know where I am," he said, as if thinking about it for the first time. There was a little frown between his baby eyebrows.

Then we saw a falling star, a long white tail trailing behind it. It fell and fell and fell. It seemed to be just the kind of star Poppa said was right for wishing on.

"Go on, Tommy," I said, a part of me wishing that Tommy wouldn't make his wish. "There's your falling star."

"I wish . . . ," said Tommy. He squeezed his eyes shut. Then he opened them and kicked the grass with the heel of his foot. "I can't do it," he said. "Some people are *supposed* to be Lonely Onlies. I think I *like* being a Lonely Only."

The sky seemed very dark all of a sudden and the stars very far away. There was no spinning ball, no white light spitting sparks of blue and red and yellow.

I knew Tommy was right—he *was* better as a Lonely Only—but there were tears in my eyes. Sammy was going to have to go home now.

Sammy looked at me and at Tommy, and Tommy and I looked at him.

"It was cool floating with you, Sammy," said Tommy. "Maybe you could come back sometime." He started to walk away. "Maybe when I get older I'll come visit you in a rocket. See you later, Allie," he said with a yawn. "I'm going back to sleep. And, hey, Allie, don't forget to open my birthday present."

"What present?" I called out to him, but he didn't hear me, and I didn't ask again.

Sammy ran toward me. As I knelt down to hug him, he clasped his baby mice fingers around my neck. "Good-bye, Allie," he said gruffly. "Say good-bye to Mom and Dad and Poppa. I think they'll understand."

Sammy took three running steps and leapt into the air. "You're a great sister," he called. "The best!"

I sat on the grass watching Sammy. He was a star falling up. I watched him until my tears made him fuzzy and I couldn't tell him apart from the other stars.

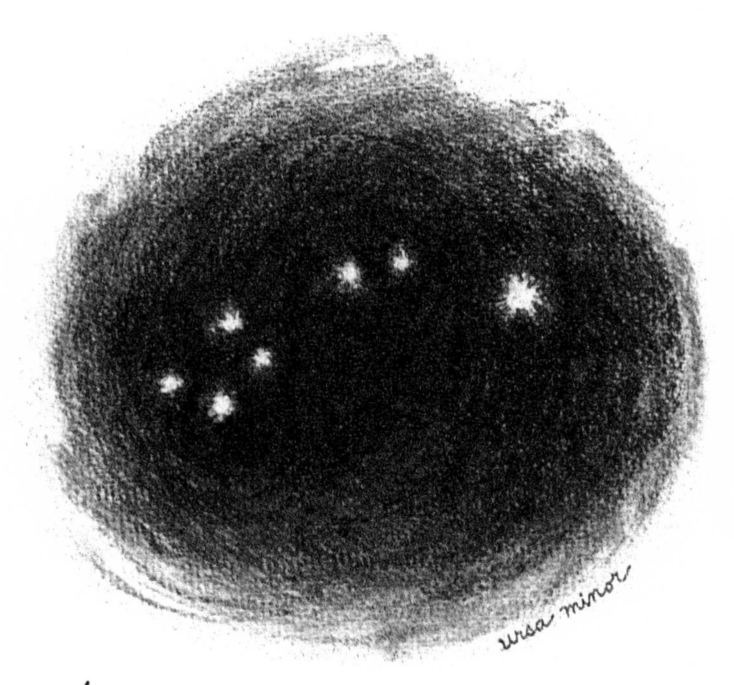

"Ten," says Poppa.

We are sitting at the table on my tenth birthday waiting for Mom to bring in my cake.

"There are ten planets that we know of," says Poppa. "Venus, Earth, Mars, Mercury, Saturn, Jupiter, Neptune, Uranus, Pluto, and the new planet X. So you see, the universe is made up of ten things."

"You left out the sun and the moon," says Dad. "Not to mention the stars and all the Star Babies."

"'What else about ten?" I ask as my brother Peter begins to cry.

Dad rocks him in his arms as if he has been holding babies forever.

"Did you know that our number system is based on ten?" asks Poppa. "It's because people have ten fingers and we've always used them to count with."

I look at Poppa's fingers, and then at Peter's — ten old moles and ten perfect baby mice.

"What else about ten?" I ask.

"In your tenth year you stopped being a Lonely Only," Mom calls from the kitchen.

"Peter won't walk as fast as Sammy did, will he?" I ask.

Dad laughs. "Not Peter. He's an Earth Baby," he says proudly.

I hadn't been sure how Dad was going to be with a baby who couldn't float or balloon up in a bath, but so far Dad has been as proud of Peter as he always has been of me.

"He'll probably bug you in much worse ways than Sammy ever did," says Poppa, rubbing a hand

across his face. "He's a Gemini. He'll be a talker. And what's more, you can't send him back."

Mom brings out the cake. "Happy birthday," everyone sings. The candles gleam in Poppa's glasses.

"Poppa," I say. "Isn't there something special that can happen to me now that I'm ten?"

"Well, let's see," he says. "There's an eclipse of the moon this month, and I believe that means if you turn ten on the ninth day of the ninth month and you make a wish just as it turns dark, you can do just about anything you want to do."

"Poppa," says Dad in a warning tone of voice.

"I'd like to be able to fly," I say, remembering the night above the fields with Sammy.

"Poppa," says Dad again, but Poppa hums his aria while Mom cuts the cake. He seems to be smiling at me as he hums.

"I'd like to be able to fly," I say again. But I whisper to Peter as his eyes flutter open, "And I'll take you with me."